MONSTER

WOF

BOOK 2

2. Nuisance to the Witches

By Priya Grewal

Chapter One

Horanio lifted her broomstick out of the rack in her cottage and happily exited her cottage to attend The Witches Annual Broomstick Race. Five years had passed since the witches and the Elders from the human planet had banished the demon monsters Sarqual and Dekrov to an underground prison for trying to enslave the human and monster races into worshipping them for all of eternity with The Red Diamond they had found. The Red Diamond was an artefact said to hold the power of all the gods. The pair of demon monsters had found it and forcibly forced every individual into worshipping them and if anyone refused, then they would torture each individual with slavery. Horanio had managed to gather all the witches and made a secret alliance with the Elders on the human planet. The witches and Elders had enough magic between them to take the Red Diamond from Sarqual and Dekrov and imprison them forever. The universe was restored and the human world and monster world had co-existed peacefully ever since. The Red Diamond was hidden away to never be found with the witches and Elders sealing it away forever magically.

Horanio had continued having a fun existence ever since the pair of demons had been imprisoned away with no magic to release them. She had enjoyed life immensely since.

Horanio smiled as she got close to the field used for The Witches Annual Broomstick Race. A few of the witches turned around and greeted her as she made her way to the participants area. There was great music playing which filled the air and magical fires reaching the sky. Horanio had signed up earlier in the year to participate in the event. She walked over to sign in for the event. Horanio said good luck to the other witches as the organiser, a witch called Slevlack told everyone participating to get in their starting positions. Horanio took her place behind the line marked out on the grass for the witches to stand behind.

"MOUNT YOUR BROOMS!" Slevlack shouted, her voice amplified by magic. The witches in the audience had formed a great circle around the race area. A stadium full of seats had also been magicked up.

Horanio excitedly mounted her broom, heart filling with anticipation.

"ON YOUR MARKS...GET SET....GO!" roared Slevlack.

Horanio commanded her broom to move. The broom began to sail higher and higher up into the air and when Horanio's head was nearly touching the clouds above, Horanio commanded her broom to move at full speed.

Full speed broom! Horanio commanded. The wind swept past Horanio's face as she urged her broom to move faster and faster. She sped ahead of many of the other contestants. She was approaching the front of the competition with only three witches in front of her.

Faster broom! Horanio commanded. Horanio's broom surged ahead. She overtook two of the contestants. She saw the one remaining contestant in front of her glance behind her at Horanio.

The witch, a red faced witch called Javaine was the only competitor in front of Horanio now. Javaine had won the previous year too.

Horanio gritted her teeth against the wind urging her broom to go faster. Horanio was almost level with Javaine.

Come on, Horanio thought to herself as the finishing line came into sight.

Horanio was almost completely level with Javaine, Horanio flying above Javaine.

The two witches were almost neck and neck. Javaine's broom crossed the finishing line with Horanio only a split second behind her.

Horanio crossed the finishing line. She came to a halt on her broom. The witches below were cheering.

"Better luck next time!" Javaine said jovially, grinning as she paused on her broom to talk to Horaino.

"It was really close though!" Javaine said and flew away on her broom heading towards the ground.

"Ah!" Horanio exclaimed. Horanio was still happy, she didn't take not winning hard. It was fun to compete in the race. She knew that Javaine had won because she practiced so hard for the race.

Horanio couldn't be bothered to practice flying at a great speed as much as Javaine but practiced more than the witches behind her.

Maybe I'll try to practice more than Javaine to win next year, Horanio thought to herself.

Second place isn't too bad, she mused to herself.

Horanio began flying on her broom towards the ground to collect her reward for coming second place.

Chapter Two

Horanio walked back to her cottage carrying her second place reward which was a statue of a broomstick which said *second place* on it. Horanio enjoyed being presented the trophy in front of all the other witches. She felt immensely proud of herself. It was now night time and the stars were shining in the night sky.

Horanio magicked her door open when she reached her cottage. She closed the door behind her. She happily placed her broomstick trophy on her mantlepiece above her living room fireplace. An open chest of drawers caught Horanio's eye. Horanio frowned. She walked up to the chest of drawers to find the draw empty. Horanio gasped.

"WHO HAS TAKEN MY JEWELS?!" Horanio cried. Everything that Horanio had been given to her as a trade for access to limited magical powers by the other monsters on Monster World had gone missing! Her drawer had been full of magnificent necklaces, rings, bracelets and more. Her favourite pair of earrings had also been stolen. The witches had decided some time ago to have a business of passing on magical powers to monsters if they gave them something in return. Horanio had always loved all the jewellery she had been given. She loved her jewels.

Horanio checked the rest of her cottage for any sign of disturbance. Everything else was in its rightful place. There was just the empty chest of drawers.

"Who would do this?" Horanio asked herself. "Who would mess with us witches when we have magical powers?" Horanio asked herself out loud.

Horanio decided she would use magic to try and see who took the jewellery. She conjured an image in front of her commanding her magic to show her who had stolen the jewellery, who was the thief?

As Horanio waited to discover who the thief was so she could exact revenge, the bubble in front of her turned black. Her magic had nothing to show her.

Horanio gasped. The culprit had blocked himself or herself from being seen! That means the culprit had access to magic so no one could find out who the thief was!

Horanio stomped furiously out of her cottage.

"WITCHES!" she shouted amplifying her voice so every witch could hear her.

Horanio waited as each witch in the village left her cottage to join her on the street.

"What's wrong?" Slevlack asked. Slevlack was in her night clothes. She rubbed her eyes. It looked like she had been disrupted from going to sleep.

The other witches stood around Horanio looking curious.

"Someone…someone.." Horanio spat. "Someone has stolen my jewellery that I had given to me by monsters for some magic in return!"

"Oh no!" Javaine said still holding her broomstick, her first place medal still around her neck.

"I used magic to show me who did it but the person blocked themselves from being seen with magic somehow!" Horanio spluttered. "I can't discover who did it!"

"Well, it can't have been anyone here!" Slevlack said. "We all have our own jewels from trading! Why would any of us need to steal anything?!"

There was a murmur of agreement around the circle of witches.

"I'm not accusing anybody here," Horanio insisted. "I'm at a loss for what I can do with the thief blocking themselves from being seen with magic somehow!"

"Everyone try and see who the thief is with their magic!" Slevlack ordered the rest.

There were murmurs of confusion as the bubble to see the past in front of every witch just showed a black bubble.

"See!" Horanio spluttered. "Like I said."

A witch with a blue face called Elezra stepped forward.

"This is indeed very strange!" Elezra announced to all.

"As we can't see who the thief is with magic, there is no point trying to do anymore now! It's night time and I'm sure everyone wants to relax in their cottage. Let's reconvene here tomorrow at 1pm for a group meeting to see what can be done about this strange happening!" Elezra ordered.

Javaine patted Horanio on the back comfortingly.

"Don't worry," Javaine said. "We'll try and get to the bottom of it tomorrow." She walked back towards her cottage.

"Sorry, nothing more can be done tonight!" Elezra said to Horanio with Slevlack standing next to her still.

"We'll try and come up with a way to discover who the thief is tomorrow. Goodnight," Elezra said walking away a moment later.

Slevlack smiled compassionately to Horanio and headed back towards her cottage.

"Hmph!" Horanio said, feeling disgruntled. She walked back into her cottage and shut the door. She put a spell on the door to make sure it was shut firmly and that no one could get in.

She attached a bell to her door and window so she would be notified if anyone did manage to get into her cottage again.

She trotted upstairs to her bedroom deciding to leave the light on, so she didn't wake up creeped out in the middle of the night!

Chapter Three

The next morning Horanio had her breakfast and boiled some water in her kettle so that she could have a cup of tea. She poured the hot water into a mug and put some milk and sugar in it. Horanio sat on her sofa by her fireplace pondering who the thief could be. She tried to think whether she had made any enemies over the years. Nothing came to mind. She got on well with all the other witches and the only dealings she had with monsters outside of The Witches Village was trading a little bit of magic for jewels most of the time.

Horanio continued staring into the fire, her mug clasped in her hands. When it was 1pm, Horanio left her cottage to reconvene with the witches.

Horanio stood outside her cottage murmuring welcome to the other witches. Javaine arrived a moment later, smiling brightly.

"How are you feeling this morning, Horanio?" Javaine asked sympathetically.

"Well, I managed to get some sleep," Horanio replied.

"But I've been trying to work out who has a grudge against me, to do this?" Horanio asked.

"A grudge?" Javaine asked. "You don't think it was just someone after your jewellery?" Javaine questioned, eyebrows raised.

"Hmm, no," replied Horanio. "Are monsters from the other villages really going to be that bothered about stealing jewellery and risking our wrath when we have our magic to scare them?" Horanio asked.

"Hmm," Javaine replied. "That's something to consider!"

Horanio turned her head to see Elezra stomping angrily towards them. She was followed by Slevlack who looked extremely concerned.

"What's wrong?" Horanio asked worriedly, not used to seeing Elezra not in her usual calm mood.

Elezra had some leaves in her hand and what looked like a part of a green shrub. She amplified her voice magically for all the witches standing in the circle to hear.

"SOMEONE!" Elezra shouted. "SOMEONE HAS DESTROYED THE SHRUBS INFRONT OF MY HOUSE!! THEY LEFT THE DESTROYED MESS THERE TOO!!" Elezra roared.

There were gasps and worried looks around the circle of witches.

"SOMEONE IS MESSING WITH US!" Elezra roared furiously, raising her fist in the air.

"Do you think it was the same person who stole my jewellery?" asked Horanio, eyes widening.

"Yes!" spat Elezra. "It must be! There is no such thing as coincidences!"

There was another murmur of agreement around the circle of witches.

"Okay," Slevlack said, looking around the circle.

"So, we're agreed? We all think the same culprit stole Horanio's jewellery and destroyed Elezra's shrubs in front of her cottage?" Slevlack asked the circle of witches.

The circle of witches all started responding with a yes.

"Anyone have any ideas who might have a grudge against us all?" Horanio asked the entire circle.

There were murmurs and head shakes, none of the witches coming up with any suggestions.

"Well, we're agreed it is no one here, as said last night," Slevlack said, "as we all have our own jewels and jewellery from trading, so doesn't make any sense. So, it could be a monster from another village. What would his or her grudge be?"

There was a silence amongst the witches.

A moment later an orange faced witch named Gladov, waved her hand in the air.

Everyone turned to look at her.

"Speak," Slevlack said to Gladov, Elezra still looking furious about her shrubs.

"Well, what if we've made a big name for ourselves in monster world with our trading a little magic for jewels and whatever else we're offered," Gladov suggested. "What if a monster got jealous of us becoming a big deal in Monster World and that's what the grudge is," Gladov suggested.

The witches started speaking amongst themselves.

Horanio considered the suggestion.

"Makes sense to me," Horanio agreed, after pondering on the suggestion for a moment.

"Monster World is MASSIVE!" Elezra complained. "How are we going to find out which monster it is behind the two crimes?!" Elezra questioned.

"Well, let's think for a moment," Slevlack intervened. "The culprit has acquired magic from somewhere to shield themselves from being seen. That means the only way to catch the monster is to set a trap for this evening. I don't think the culprit would dare do anything in the day!" Slevlack instructed them all.

"What trap do we set?" asked Elezra.

"Hmm," Horanio pondered. "If we're all in our cottages by 6pm this evening we could set an alarm to go off if an intruder who isn't a witch comes into the village," Horanio suggested. "Then we could set up a net using magic to catch the monster automatically as soon as the alarm goes off."

"Sounds good," Elezra said, determinedly.

"Everyone in agreement to be in their cottages by 6pm and is everyone happy with the plan?" Slevlack asked all the witches.

The circle of witches said yes and nodded their heads.

"Right," Elezra said, turning to Horanio. "Let's set that trap!"

Chapter Four

Horanio sat on her sofa by her fireplace waiting for the clock to strike 6. Herself, Elezra and Slevlack had set up the alarm and net to capture the monster who had stolen Horanio's jewellery and destroyed Elezra's shrubs. Horanio waited nervously. The clock struck 6pm. Elezra stared at her clock as it chimed to let her know it was 6pm.

"Here we go," Horanio muttered to herself. She had closed her curtains too, as had all the witches so the monster who was behind the crimes, would feel confident about coming into the village. Horanio stared at her clock for the next half an hour. She was getting more and more fidgety waiting for something to happen. All of a sudden, as the clock struck 6:30pm, the loud alarm sounded, the noise reaching every witch in her cottage. Horanio abruptly left her seat and exited her cottage to have a look at the monster who had been captured. Horanio rushed over to the net which was at the centre of the village. Horanio looked at the net in dismay.

"What...," Horanio murmured to herself, as she stared at the net. The other witches had arrived and were gathered around the net as well, all of them looking dismayed.

The net had five grey rocks in it. Horanio glanced up to see Elezra staring at the rocks and looking furious.

Slevlack briefly put her arm around Horanio comfortingly.

"How is this possible?" Slevlack asked, with a confused look on her face.

"It means that the monster has access to magic somehow and foresaw that we had set a trap and magicked some grey rocks in the net instead. He or she is probably laughing at us as we speak," Elezra exclaimed furiously.

"There's only two ways for a monster to obtain magic," Gladov chirped in, cleverly. "The only two sources in the universe that can give out magic is ourselves the witches, or the Elders from the human planet, who we worked with in the past to imprison Dekrov and Sarqual," Gladov added.

Everyone was silent for a moment.

"Well, no one here would give out magic to do this," Javaine piped up. "There isn't a motive!"

"This could lead to war with the Elders if it continues," Elezra added in.

"Now, now," Slevlack said calmly. "It doesn't mean the Elders knew what the magic the monster used to conceal themselves was for. The monster could have bribed one of the Elders and the Elders didn't ask any questions," Slevlack added.

There were murmurs around the circle of witches, all looking confused.

Next, the sound of glass tinkling reached the ears of the witches.

"What was that?" Slevlack inquired, abruptly.

Elezra frowned.

"Show us," Elezra commanded her magic. A large purple arrow protruded from Elezra's finger and showed the witches which direction to walk in.

The witches all began walking as a crowd in the direction the arrow pointed them to. They suddenly came to a halt in front of Slevlack's cottage.

All of the witches gasped. Slevlack pushed her way to the front of the crowd.

"What is this?" Slevlack roared. Slevlack's window had been smashed with a rock! The rock could be seen on the other side of the window in Slevlack's living room. Horanio returned Slevlack's comfort by tapping her on the back briefly.

"The monster was here," Elezra said, dramatically. "He or she went to smash the windows as we looked at the net," Elezra added in.

"Show yourself!" Horanio shouted. Nothing happened.

The witches all looked scared.

"I won't rest," Slevlack said, "until we have caught the culprit. He or she will not get away with terrorizing our village!" Slevlack pledged.

A short while later, all the witches had agreed to pair up and stay at one another's cottage for the night, so no witch was by herself. They all felt uneasy staying in their cottages by themselves with the terrorizing monster out there somewhere.

Horanio had paired up with Elezra. The pair walked solemnly back to Horanio's cottage.

"I don't like this," Elezra said to Horanio. "I don't like this one bit. Feeling gripped with fear for the evening with a monster out there somewhere, with a grudge against us," Elezra confided.

"I know," Horanio agreed. "We're going to have to come up with something to deal with this monster."

Chapter Five

Elezra and Horanio were sat on the sofas around the fireplace in Horanio's cottage. Both of them clasped mugs of tea in their hands. It was around 9pm.

"What can we do to trap the monster for real this time?" Elezra asked Horanio. "There's no point setting up a plan with all the witches as the monster can look in and see what we're doing, using magic," Elezra complained.

"Hmm...," Horanio pondered for a moment. "Let's block ourselves from being seen with magic so no one can look in on us either."

"Okay," Elezra responded more brightly. "And then...?"

"Hmm," Horanio pondered again. "Then we can go outside invisibly and set the same trap again, this time without him or her knowing," Horanio suggested.

"Good plan!" Elezra exclaimed, enthusiastically.

"Let's do it!" Elezra exclaimed. Both witches briefly started chanting so that no one could look into their conversation, using magic. They cast a spell so that anyone looking in magically would see an alternative conversation with the pair merely sitting on the sofas for the evening, as opposed to copying the black bubble the monster used, which might arouse suspicion of them planning anything.

"Okay, the spell is cast," Horanio said. "We have our cover!"

"Now what?" Elezra asked Horanio.

"Let's turn invisible and go outside. I'll make it so no one can see the door open," Horanio quickly started chanting a spell again.

Horanio and Elezra both made themselves invisible. They walked over to the door and opened it. Due to Horanio's magic, anyone watching wouldn't see the door open to become suspicious.

Horanio and Elezra both started chanting in their heads to re-set the same trap with an alarm and net again.

"Now let's wait," Horanio said to Elezra telepathically, not wanting to make a sound.

The pair of witches waited in the dark, their insides filling with anticipation and some fear.

Nothing happened for a while.

"I'm going to cast a spell so that the net turns any invisible entity visible for us to see," Horanio told Elezra telepathically.

"Good thinking," Elezra replied back.

Horanio silently commanded the net to turn any intruder caught visible, in case the monster too was invisible.

Horanio and Elezra waited and waited in silence. It was nearing midnight.

Suddenly, at a quarter to midnight, the alarm was set off and it could be loudly heard across the village, waking up many of the sleeping witches.

Horanio gasped, "Let's go!" she said to Elezra. Horanio and Elezra rushed over to where they had placed the net near the centre of the village.

Horanio's eyes widened in dismay again as they reached a net and saw a horrible looking monster demon with large horns and large fangs protruding from his mouth. He also had a third eye in his forehead.

Horanio amplified her voice in triumph.

"WE HAVE CAUGHT THE MONSTER!" Horanio shouted victoriously for all to hear.

"YES!" Elezra shouted, happily.

The other witches began to gather around the net with the monster in.

He had some golden goblets and plates in his hands.

Gladov made her way to the front of the crowd.

"HEY!" Gladov shouted. "Those are mine!"

Gladov magically slapped the monster without physically touching him.

"OW!" the monster growled. "GET ME OUT OF THIS NET!" the monster roared.

"I forgot to cast a spell on my door to keep intruders out," Gladov told them all. "I went to bed. He must have snuck in then!"

"Maybe he used magic on you to forget," Horanio said.

"He must have been able to teleport in as he didn't set off the alarm on the way in!" Horanio said.

"Who are you?" Elezra shouted at the monster demon.

"What is your name?" Elezra asked the monster demon.

The monster demon growled unhappily.

"My name is Rozro," the monster demon said, knowing there was no point in lying as he had been caught.

"Which village are you from?" Horanio asked the monster demon.

"I'm of the horned folk demon species," the monster demon replied, "with extra eyes."

"And why have you been terrorizing our village, stealing, smashing windows and destroying shrubs?" asked Horanio.

'Because I felt like it," the monster demon replied.

Horanio waved her hands and green magic left her hands, raising the monster demon Rozro high into the air.

"I hope you know there's no way of you leaving the net," Horanio told Rozro.

"Now where did you get the magic from? Who provided you with the MAGIC?" Horanio demanded to know.

The monster demon fell silent.

"TELL ME!" Horanio roared again. The other witches looked at the scene eyes wide.

"I don't know," Rozro responded. "Whenever I try to remember my mind goes blank!"

Horanio turned to look at Elezra in exasperation.

"I'll me back in a moment!" Elezra whispered to Horanio leaving the circle and walking away.

"WHY HAVE YOU BEEN TERRORIZING US?" Horanio demanded to know.

"Because I felt like it," Rozro responded again.

"What grudge do you have?" Gladov shouted to the monster.

The monster Rozro grinned, not saying anything.

Gladov sent a magical slap to the monster again. His face whipped around for a moment in response to the slap.

"OW!" Rozro shouted to Gladov.

"WAIT UNTIL I GET OUT OF HERE!" he roared.

"You're not getting out of the net," Horanio told the monster.

Rozro fell silent. He started grinning at the witches again.

"Wipe that grin off your face!" Slevlack ordered. "You've been caught!"

"That's right!" Javaine added in. The monster looked at Javaine and then looked away, still looking mischievous.

The witches watched the monster in silence for a few moments, deciding what they should do with him.

A few moments later Elezra returned.

"I have to tell everyone something," Elezra whispered into Horanio's ear.

"What is it?" Horanio asked, furrowing her eyebrows in confusion.

Elezra made her way to the centre of the circle, standing next to the monster demon Rozro in his net.

"THERE IS A TRAITOR AMONG US!" roared Elezra. "A WITCH HERE IN OUR VILLAGE IS IN LEAGUE WITH THIS MONSTER DEMON AND IS IN PARTNERSHIP WITH HIMSELF TO AFFLICT OUR VILLAGE WITH THESE CRIMES AND TERROR!" Elezra told the shocked circle.

Elezra looked furious.

"AND THAT TRAITOR IS...," Elezra shouted, "JAVAINE!"

The witches all gasped and one by one turned to look at Javaine who was leaving the front of the circle trying to get to the back.

"TRAITOR!" Slevlack screamed pointing to Javaine.
Javaine stopped in her tracks turning to face the circle.

Chapter Six

Horanio gasped as shocked as the other witches. Elezra quickly clicked her fingers and Javaine was caught in a net. Elezra then levitated the net with Javaine inside of it, so she was hanging in the air like Rozro.

"There," Elezra shouted to Javaine. "Now you can't use magic to escape!"

Javaine said nothing and stared furiously at Elezra, her eyes beginning to show malice.

Elezra turned to address the circle of witches.

"I got suspicious!" Elezra told the other witches. "How could the monster have known we were setting up a trap and put rocks in the net himself! Someone must have told him. Someone who was probably on the inside. It didn't make sense for the Elders to have a grudge against us to give a monster that much magic, to teleport in and turn invisible!"

"I felt suspicious of there being a traitor as I sat in Horanio's cottage this evening, thinking to myself," Elezra stated.

"I didn't want to say anything without having proof, the thought newly formed in my mind," Elezra explained. "And obviously I didn't know who to trust at that point with telling them anything!"

The witches stared at Elezra in silence, looking shocked.

"So, I slipped away just now. Javaine had blocked her and the monster from being seen with magic. So, I looked for a loophole as the same black bubble came up when I tried to find out who Rozro was working with," Elezra asked.

"Instead, I asked my magic to show me who in the village was friends with Rozro, and it showed me Javaine!"

Everyone gasped again in the circle of witches. Rozro looked solemn in his net for the first time.

"I wanted more proof, so I went to Javaine's cottage where she had left the door open! And I found THIS!" Elezra reached into her jacket pocket and pulled out a silver necklace with a red ruby and Horanio's favourite pair of earrings!

"That's some of the jewellery that was stolen from me!" Horanio exclaimed in shock.

'We split it between us both," Rozro, the monster said, as if he were finding it all amusing.

'She put magic on Rozro so he wouldn't mention her name just in case he was ever caught!" Elezra told the crowd.

Elezra zapped Rozro with some magic, undoing Javaine's spell.

"Oh yeah," Rozro finally said. "Javaine told me to do it!"

"SHUT IT!" Javaine roared.

"I'm going to zap him again to tell us the whole truth!" Elezra told the other witches.

Elezra zapped the monster demon again.

"Basically...," Rozro began "I visited Javaine who I had been friendly with in the past. She had given me some magic to grow some horrible looking mushrooms around a monster's cottage whom I didn't like. He beat me once in a race," Rozro told them all.

"I decided to visit Javaine after I had grown the mushrooms and watched the monster look all bewildered," Rozro told them all. "I thought she would find it funny when I told her to look at the scene magically."

The witches stared at Rozro, listening to every word. He seemed to enjoy them hanging off his every word for a moment.

"And then after grinning mischievously," Rozro told them all. "Javaine told me she was jealous of some of the witches here. She said that she had won The Annual Witches Broomstick Race last year and would probably win this year too with practicing but didn't get the respect that other witches here had," Rozro told them all. "She said she was jealous of Horanio, Elezra, Slevlack and Gladov for the respect that they had from the other witches. She was jealous because she didn't seem to get the same kind of respect. She said she just gloated a lot about winning and became less popular that way. So,

she wanted me to come in here and cause mischief and steal from you and break windows, as she would get a power trip from it all, with you other witches being more respected and well liked than herself. She convinced me by saying I would be invisible and there was no way to be caught because she was going to use magic to conceal ourselves, so none of you could check who the culprit was. So, I stole from Horanio, destroyed Elezra's shrubs, smashed Slevlack's window and Javaine put magic on Gladov to forget to seal her door magically and I stole these goblets from her too! I can't believe I got caught!" Rozro told them all.

The witches stared at Rozro and Javaine in shocked silence.

"My motive," Rozro declared to the witches, "was jealousy. I was jealous of the name you witches were making for yourself from trading magic for jewels etc so I said yes to doing this! I want to be respected and have a name like you all have!" Rozro declared.

Rozro fell silent, finishing his revelation.

Elezra looked at Javaine.

"Is this all true?" Elezra asked Javaine. "Well, obviously it is I zapped him to tell us the whole truth!" Elezra answered her own question.

Javaine's eyes gleamed with complete malice now.

"YES! IT'S TRUE!" she spluttered. "I was sick of you all getting respect and everyone liking you all and always speaking respectfully about yourselves. No one cared about me after winning The Witches Annual Broomstick Race! The attention you all got should have been mine! I barely had any friends left from gloating about it!" Javaine confessed. "So, I just thought I'd have a little fun with you all! Rozro here likes getting up to mischief, so I thought I'd ask him. He said he was jealous of the reputation of the witches in Monster World so gladly agreed to do the crimes I made up for him to do," Javaine confessed to them all.

"Nearly got away with it all too!" Javaine spluttered, nothing but malice in her eyes.

The witches fell silent.

"You're a coward and a traitor!" Elezra shouted to Javaine.

The rest of the witches started cheering and jeering.

"Okay," Horanio addressed all the witches, calling for silence.

"Let us gather together away from these two and decide what we want to do with them! They can't leave their nets!" Horanio told them all.

The witches all left the circle to decide what to do with the pair together.

Horanio walked to join them, shocked at the betrayal and at having a traitor amongst their midst who wished harm on them all.

Chapter Seven

The witches reached a verdict and gathered again around the nets with the criminal pair inside of them. The witches had asked Horanio to declare the verdict to the pair of criminals.

"For your malice and betrayal against us all," Horanio declared to the two criminals, "You, Javaine will be banished from our village to live by yourself in another dimension. You will not be allowed to inflict us with any more harm. You are a truly dreadful and horrible being and it will be a happier village and world without you in it!" Horanio told Javaine.

"Noooooooooo!" Javaine screamed. "I don't want to live alone forever!! I'm sorry," she pleaded. "He lied, he made me do it, I swear," Javaine pleaded.

'And you will be stripped of your magical powers," Horanio told Javaine. Horanio began draining Javaine of her magic using her own magic.

"Nooooooooo! Please!" Javaine screeched in her net.

Elezra smiled victoriously at Javaine.

"Slevlack ,would you do the honours, please," Elezra asked.

 "Sure," Slevlack replied getting her hands ready. Slevlack began to open a big circular portal in the air. A vortex span within the circular portal.

"Bye, bye!" Elezra shouted happily.

With her magic Elezra, pushed Javaine into the circular portal and it closed up a split second later, sealing Javaine the traitor, away forever.

"Good riddance to bad rubbish!" Elezra said happily. The witches in the circle all started clapping and cheering.

"As for you," Horanio said sternly, turning to address Rozro.

"You will be given the same punishment. Sent to another dimension to live by yourself forever with no access to magic of course!" Horanio told the criminal monster.

"Noooooooooo!" shouted Rozro. "Not by myself forever! Please I'll do anything!" Rozro begged.

"And again please, Slevlack," Horanio requested. Slevlack lifted her hands in the air and opened another circular portal with a vortex spinning on the inside.

"Off you go, Rozro!" Elezra exclaimed happily, lifting her hands and magically pushing Rozro into the empty dimension to live by himself forever. The portal sealed itself closed a moment later.

A split second later, the witches all started cheering. The criminals were caught and disposed of. Their village was at peace again.

The witches all lifted Horanio and Elezra onto their shoulders celebrating themselves for catching the culprit. Horanio was lifted up in celebration for setting the trap again and Elezra was lifted in celebration for discovering that Javaine was the traitor in their midst and even that there was a traitor at all.

The witches carried the pair and set off fireworks in the air to celebrate the demise of the criminals.

The Witches Village was at peace again.

Chapter Eight

Horanio sat on her favourite seat by her fireplace that evening, sipping tea happily.

She rested her head back on the seat and said, "Ahhhh, back to normal at last."

Horanio closed her eyes for a moment happily and then reached out her hands to warm herself with the lit fire in her fireplace!

THE END.

Printed in Great Britain
by Amazon